My Little Artist

My Little Artist

WRITTEN AND
ILLUSTRATED BY

Donna Green

SMITHMARK

This edition published in 1999 by SMITHMARK Publishers,
A division of U.S. Media Holdings, Inc.
115 West 18th Street, New York, NY 10011; (212) 519-1300

SMITHMARK books are available for bulk purchase
for sales promotions and premium use.
For details write to the manager of special sales,
SMITHMARK Publishers, A division of U.S. Media Holdings, Inc.
115 West 18th Street, New York, NY 10011; (212) 519-1300

My Little Artist
Produced by VIA
c/o Vermilon, Inc. / PO Box 485
Marshfield, MA 02050, USA

A Rob Fremont Book

Designed by Carol Belanger Grafton

Printed and bound in Singapore by Imago Publishing Ltd.

Library of Congress Cataloging-in-Publication Data

Green, Donna
   My little artist / written and illustrated by Donna Green
      p.   cm.
   Summary: A grandmother shares her vision of being an artist and
      teaches her granddaughter to see the world with "heartsight."
   ISBN 0-7651-1742-8 (hardcover)
   [1. Grandmothers Fiction. 2. Artists Fiction] I. Title.
   P27.G8196Mt   1999
   [E]—dc21   99-20004
                                                      CIP

2   4   6   8   10   9   7   5   3   1

For those who have an artist
within: trust your "heartsight!"

Hurrying down the path through my grandparents' orchard I pass the stump where Grandma would braid my hair each morning. I can still feel her soft hands going back and forth at a slow rhythmic pace that told me how much she loved me. "Oh, you have pretty hair," she would say. "It sparkles like the meadow creek in the morning." As my feet splash over polished stones, I recall our favorite game: "Study, Compare, and Remember." Everything she taught me had common ground with something I already understood. Grandma fueled my curiosity with intriguing snippets of wisdom wherever we went, and in the magical light of her garden, taught me the meaning of heartsight.

"Grandma, how do I become an artist? I want to be just like you."

"Well, I guess that depends on your heartsight."

"Oh Grams, you're teasing me. There's no such thing."

"Remember . . . my little artist, our eyes see only the surface; our hearts look at the world from the inside out. An artist who has heartsight can capture light."

I thought for a moment. "That sounds hard, Grandma."

She just smiled.

"Tell me how you see the trees," Grandma would say. "Close your eyes and imagine the light as it dances through the branches and onto your face. What makes them move in your mind? Can you feel the birds flying? Can you smell the sunlight as it falls to earth?"

"How do I become an artist?" I'd ask.

"Heartsight!" she would sing.

"Mrs. Wren was adding fluffy stuff to her nest. I sneaked up and saw three little eggs. They weren't there yesterday. Do you think they felt me watching?"

"Maybe so," whispered Grandma.

"Have you ever noticed how butterflies seem to defy gravity?"

I sat quietly as a pretty little

spot turned into a Flutterby

In the garden while I was pretending to ride on the back of a turtle, Grandma asked if I could catch the sun bouncing off, glimmering on, or peeking through, some of my favorite hideaways. Light became magic . . .

and I wanted to PLay with it.

"Grandma, how many baby peas are there in one mommy pod?"

"Many, I imagine. When the sun comes out from behind the clouds we can count them. One . . . two . . . three . . .."

"I see nine! Do you think they kick like real babies?"

"How do you catch the light, Grandma?"

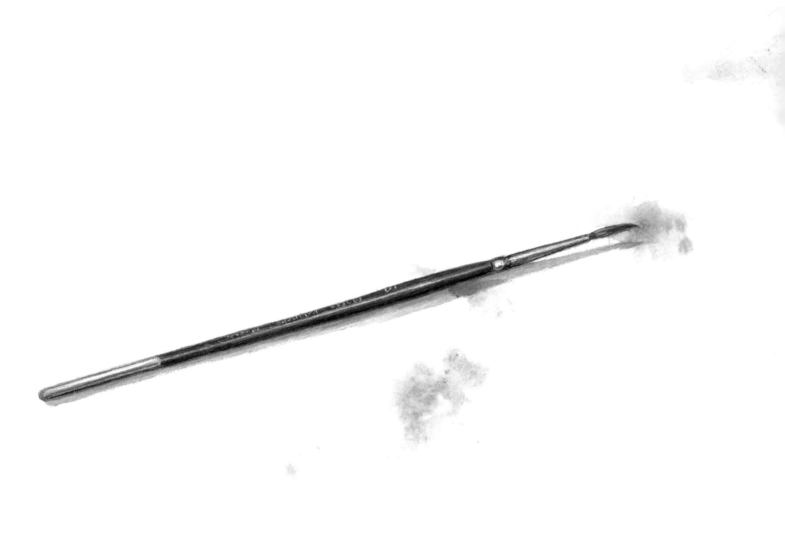

I sipped on sweet tea and honey as my grandma's fingers danced over paper. Her paint brush dipped and splashed until, just like magic, a cupful of sunshine appeared.

"Did you know only the sweetest-tasting raspberries make your chin turn red? Hold one under my chin to see if it glows."

"Who gets to taste-test them?" asked Grandma.

"We can take turns," I promised.

Mr. Grouse

"Mr. Grouse likes the mushy ones. He's been waiting under the bushes."

We giggled as tadpoles tickled our toes and Grandma made the frogpond look like a giant mirror. Sometimes she would say, "It's only when we look below the surface that we really understand what we are seeing."

I slowly began to realize the art lessons Grandma gave me were truly lessons in life. She taught me that without experiencing my life in dimension, my art would also be flat.

"I wonder why the sunshine wiggles on the walk.
Maybe the bricks are taking turns talking.
Now I'm in the light. It's my turn!"

Grandma and I sat on her feather bed daydreaming as lacy shapes flew with the wind around her room.

"How does the sun put your curtains over there?" I asked.

"The sun knows about heartsight," answered Grandma with a twinkle.

"Oh Grams," I thought.

Study, Compare, and remember

"Look, I found a new friend. His eyes are the color of Mom's pea soup. I don't think I'll introduce him to Mr. Grouse, though. Mr. Grouse can eat the raspberries."

"Why are you dipping your paper into water?"
I asked at the sink.

"I want a sky as blue as your eyes. When I drop
my paint onto the wet paper it explodes just
like my heart does for you."

Drop by drop the color exploded into a glorious
sky then slowly dripped off the edge and seemed to
disappear as the wet paper soaked up the color.

"Oh Grandma, it was so beautiful, but now it's gone!"

"Sweetheart, all things fade with time. It's the moment-to-moment living that we mustn't lose sight of. A piece of white paper can carry us anywhere as long as we're not afraid to leave."

"Grams, next time I'm going to add the color of your eyes to the color of mine!"

"Grandma, I drew a picture for you. It's of an angel sliding down a moonbeam. She has pretty rainbow wings just like the dragonfly in our garden. The moonlight is turning into sparkles and they move like the curtains in your room! Remember? GRANDMA!"

"Yes, love," said Grandma with happy tears. "Heartsight!

My little artist found her heartsight!"

And she gave me one of her big Grandma hugs!

Standing here now in the sweet-smelling attic of her cottage, I proudly hold my first published book.

"Grandma, this moment is ours," I whisper.

Frosted breath magnifies the stillness of the room as I yearn for just one more hug. Reaching up for an old photograph of Grandma, I accidentally cause a few of her treasures to fall from a shelf. In a sliver of moonlight, a piece of yellowing paper floats down like a weightless butterfly and gently lands at my feet. As I pick up my drawing of the angel, Grandma's words wrap around me like a warm quilt: "All things are possible with heartsight, my love."